This book is dedicated to my amazing wife Lakeisha and our three sons Isaiah, 14, Taylor, 9, and Liam 3

The foundation we share is what makes me the man I am today. So, to my beautiful wife Lakeisha Palmer, thanks for loving me and allowing me to lead our family. You are the true representation of what a wife and mother looks like and I wake up honored everyday knowing that God allowed me to marry his daughter.

"Acknowledging the good that you already have in your life is the foundation for all abundance."

ISBN: 9780578820361

Hi, everyone. I'm Liam and I have a story to tell. My potty training is an adventure filled with ups and downs, funny situations and one wonderful miracle.

You see, not too long ago, Dad tried everything to get me to go potty on my own. Every day, Dad tried to show me how to do it, but I was just too used to my diapers. He tried giving me grown-up underwear, stickers and treats, but nothing was working.

SQUAT
Change

With a big smile on my face, I just went potty in my diaper and watched Dad let out a big sigh. He was so discouraged and frustrated. Dad can't stay mad at me for long, because when I laugh, he always laughs too. Just a smile from me and he can't help but laugh.

Once I heard him tell Mom, "I can't do it. Whatever I try, it doesn't work."
"Don't lose hope honey, he'll learn sooner or later. Just don't give up. Try again and again and Liam will get it in no time," she said.

Week after week, it started to look hopeless, but one day everything changed. One beautiful morning, I woke up in my bed and saw my dad carrying something in his arms and he was walking towards me. It was a bunny! He asked me to name my new pet. I told him his name was CT and smiled so big. Ever since that day, he is my best friend.

ZZZ
ZZ
Z

Now, CT and I have had all kinds of adventures together. At night, when my mom and dad are asleep, we turn into superheroes. We either go to help save the world or visit some amazing places!

Out of all our incredible adventures, today is the most exciting one so far. It's time for my potty training adventure to the golden pot! CT says, "Tonight's adventure will be a lifetime change for you Liam."

Tonight, after Mom and Dad go to bed, CT and I will put our superhero suits on right away and head out. But first...

SQUAT
for
Change
X

"Liam," he says, "I have something to tell you. I love our adventures, but if we are going to have even better and more exciting ones, you have to be potty trained. You are a big boy now and big boys don't need diapers.

If you don't need to be changed every day, just think of all the things we can do and all the places we can go to. Then after you are potty trained, we can roam the world all night long!"

SQUAT
for
Change

That sounds great! "You're right, CT, but I just can't get it right. My dad tries to teach me every day, but it's just so hard to do it. You never had diapers, CT. How did you do it?"

SQUAT
for
Change

"Well, it's easy, Liam. I can tell when I need to pee or poo, and then run to the grass to do it."

"So should I do it in the grass too?" I ask and we both start to giggle.

"No, silly. You are going to do it on the golden potty tonight!" CT says. "You little jokester."

"Golden potty?" Liam says. Yes, we are getting ready to go to the golden potty in Egypt, this country has the best golden potties in the world!

"Are you ready?" CT asks.

"Wow! Cool!" I said. "Let's go!
Hereee- weee- goooooooo!
Boom-!-Bamb-! Eyes
close and poof!"

"Welcome to the Golden Potty Museum!"

I look at CT with a big smile and glazed eyes. We both say, "WOWWW!!"

As we start walking through the potty museum, I stop and say, "Oh, CT! I think it's coming. I need to pee now!"

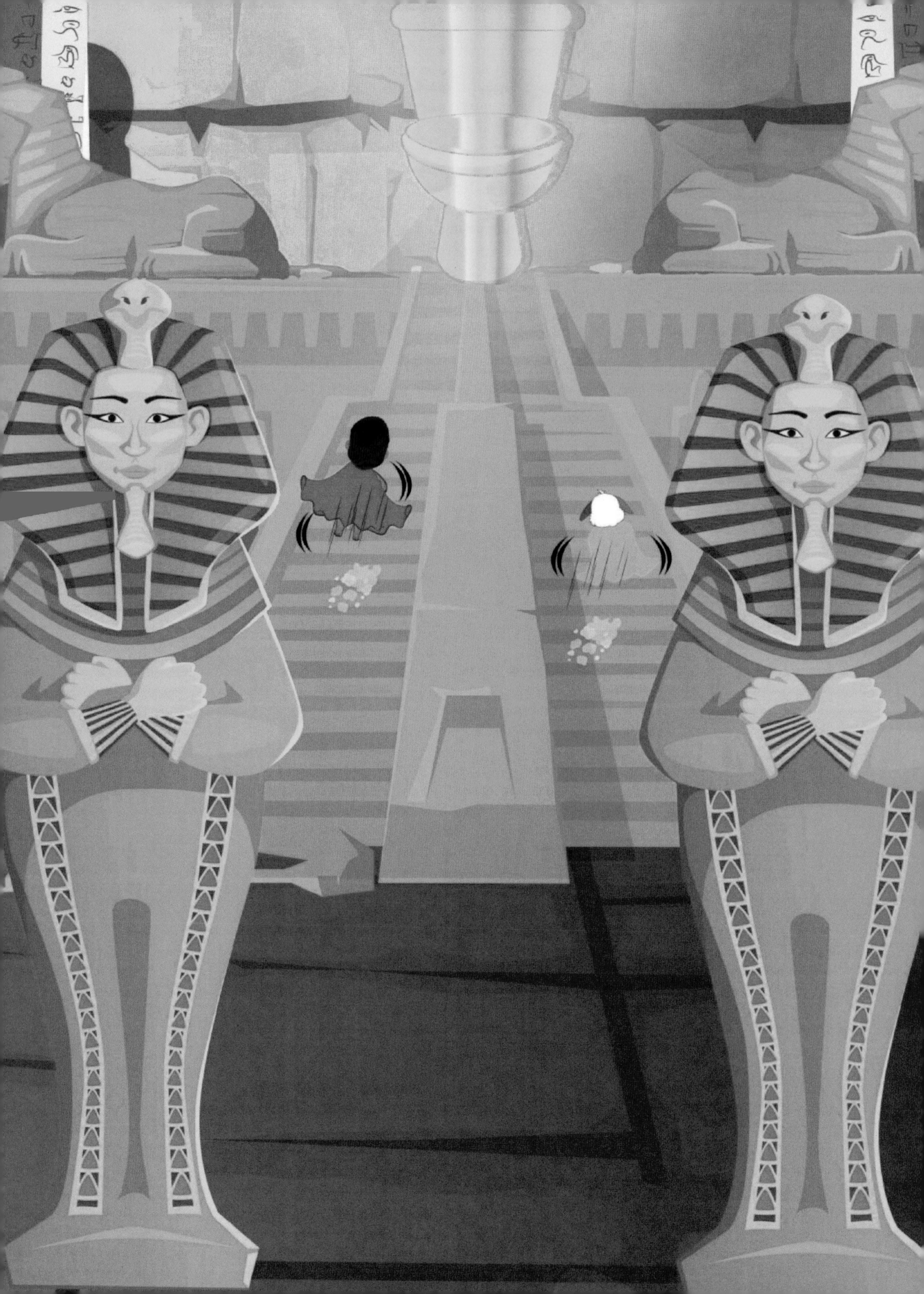

“Let’s go!” CT says and runs to the golden potty. “Look, this is how you do it!” the bunny says and crouches above the potty.

“Stop making me laugh, CT, I have to go now!” I tell him, take off my diaper and sit on the potty. I let go and just a few seconds later, I’m done.

“You did it, Liam!” CT says. “I knew you could!”

SQUAT
for
Change

I smile big and Boom-!-Bamb-! Eyes closed and poof!! Back in my bathroom at home.

SQUAT for Change

Then, we go back to my bedroom, but there's a problem.

"Oh, CT, my diaper is undone, what are we going to do?"

"Uh…" CT is looking around. "Well, I guess I'll learn to be a parent now," he says, and we start to giggle again.

When Mom and Dad do it, changing diapers looks so easy, but CT and I can't figure it out.

But then, CT grabs one end of the diaper and says, "Hey, this is sticky!" "That's how you do it, yes! My dad tapes the two sides to my diaper!" I say and CT helps me with the diaper before I get into my bed, so mom and dad won't find out about our adventure tonight.

ZZZ
ZZ
Z

It's time to get some sleep before the morning comes. But before I know it........

I’m opening my eyes and Dad is giving me a big smile.

“Good morning,” he says. “Goo—” Oh, I forgot, not good morning, I mean… “Mor-n-inggg!”

“There’s my boy!” Dad says. “Let’s see your diaper, big boy. Oh, you’re dry! You did it, Liam, you waited for me. Come on, quick, let’s go to the potty.”

SQUAT
for
Change

Dad picks me up and carries me to the potty. I do my thing just like CT taught me in Egypt and Dad is so happy!

“I did it, honey, I did it!” he calls my mom over. Mom is smiling from ear to ear!

“He went in the potty?” Mom asks with a big smile on her face, and they start dancing and jumping around.

SQUAT

They are so happy! Giggling to myself
I think, "I'll ever tell them it was the
bunny who taught me!"

But that doesn't matter because
now that I'm potty trained, the
exciting adventures can finally start.
CT and I can't wait!

THE END